D1006058

An I Can Read Book®

# Clara and the Bookwagon

## Nancy Smiler Levinson
## illustrations by Carolyn Croll

WITHDRAWN

HarperTrophy®
*A Division of* HarperCollins*Publishers*

*This book is dedicated to librarians everywhere
and to all children who are discovering
the joy of books!*

*With acknowledgment to Nina Ignatowicz,
Linda Zuckerman, Clyde Robert Bulla,
and Sue Alexander.*

HarperCollins®, ✒®, Harper Trophy®, and I Can Read Book®
are trademarks of HarperCollins Publishers Inc.

Clara and the Bookwagon
Text copyright © 1988 by Nancy Smiler Levinson
Illustrations copyright © 1988 by Carolyn Croll
All rights reserved. No part of this book may be
used or reproduced in any manner whatsoever without
written permission except in the case of brief quotations
embodied in critical articles and reviews. Printed in
the United States of America. For information address
HarperCollins Children's Books, a division of
HarperCollins Publishers, 195 Broadway,
New York, NY 10007.

*Library of Congress Cataloging-in-Publication Data*
Levinson, Nancy Smiler.
  Clara and the bookwagon.

  (An I can read book)
  Summary: Clara's dream of enriching her rough life on
the family farm is fulfilled when a horse-drawn book-
wagon visits with the country's first traveling library.
  [1. Libraries, Traveling—Fiction. 2. Books and
reading—Fiction. 3. Farm life—Fiction] I. Croll,
Carolyn, ill. II. Title. III. Title: Clara and the
book wagon. IV. Series.
PZ7.L5794C1 1987     [E]       86-45773
ISBN 0-06-023837-2
ISBN 0-06-023838-0 (lib. bdg.)
ISBN 0-06-444134-2 (pbk.)

15 16 17 18 PC/WOR 30 29 28 27 26 25

# Contents

1   On the Farm            4

2   A Trip to Town         20

3   The Black Wagon        38

4   Books for Clara        50

# 1   On the Farm

Clara lived on a small farm
in Maryland.

She helped feed the chickens.

She helped Mama cook stew.

She helped take care of
little Hans and baby Ann.

In the spring she worked
side by side with Papa
planting corn.

Clara did not go to school.

There were no schools

for farm children.

But Clara wanted to learn.

She wanted to learn about

the sun and the stars.

She wanted to learn

how corn grew from seeds.

But most of all

she wanted to learn to read.

Once after church

Reverend Strong showed Clara

his family Bible.

"What a big Bible!" Clara said.

"And what wonderful stories,"

said Reverend Strong.

Clara loved to hear stories!
She loved to hear them
told in church every Sunday.

9

Sometimes she liked
to make up her own stories.
Some were about animals.
Some were about families.
And some were about a farm girl
just like herself.
If only I could read stories,
she thought.
If only I had

a storybook of my own.

But there was no money

for extra things.

Sometimes Clara got tired of

doing farm work.

Then she would lie in the grass,

or rock in the rocking chair

Papa had carved,

and dream.

11

One day Clara was helping

Mama bake bread.

"Mama," she asked,

"how does bread rise

in the oven?"

"Oh, dear," Mama said.

"I cannot tell you now.

I am too busy."

Clara opened the oven door

to take a peek.

"Close the door, Clara,"

said Mama,

"or the bread will not rise."

"Yes, Mama," said Clara.

She sat down

in the rocking chair.

Back and forth she rocked,

back and forth.

She thought about
the bread dough.
She thought about it
rising and rising
until it popped through
the oven door.
Clara laughed to herself.

The kitchen door opened.

It was Papa.

He looked hot and tired.

His boots were dusty.

"Are you dreaming again?"

he asked Clara.

"Yes, Papa," she said.

"There is no time for dreaming

on a farm," said Papa.

"Everyone must help,

or we will have no food

on our table."

"Yes, Papa," said Clara.

Little Hans ran into the kitchen.

"Eat, eat," he cried.

"It is not dinnertime yet,"

said Mama.

"Come, Hans," said Clara.

"We will set the table.

Then I will tell you a story."

"I will go out to chop

some wood," said Papa.

"Good," said Mama.

"By that time

dinner will be ready."

## 2　A Trip to Town

Clara and Mama

were scrubbing clothes.

"Mama! Clara!" Papa called.

"I have to go into town.

We need more corn seed."

"We need flour and sugar, too,"

Mama said.

"Can I go with you?" asked Clara.

"I promise to help."

Papa smiled.

"Come along then," he said.

Clara helped Papa

hitch the horse to the wagon.

Town was a long way off—
almost seven miles.

"We will be back by sundown,"
Papa told Mama.

Mama waved good-bye.

Hans waved good-bye.

Baby Ann cried.

Clop, clop, clop.

The horse plodded along.

The sun was warm.

The spring air smelled good.

Clara and Papa rode

until they came to a stream.

"This looks like a good spot

to rest," said Papa.

He pulled the wagon to a stop.

Clara ran to the stream

and cupped her hands to drink

the clear, cool water.

"How good this tastes, Papa,"

said Clara.

Papa took a drink

and splashed water on his face.

"It feels good, too," he said.

Then Papa gave the horse a drink.

"Papa, do you know what else

would taste good?" Clara asked.

"What?" said Papa.

"A peppermint stick!" said Clara.

"A trip to town

would not be the same

without a candy treat,"

Papa said.

Clara and Papa climbed back
in the wagon and rode on.
At last they came to town.
Mr. Holzer greeted them
at the store.

"Nice weather we are having,"

he said.

"Yes," said Papa.

"Good weather for planting."

Clara looked around the store.

There was thread for sewing.

There were pots for cooking.

There were tools for building.

Then Clara saw the books.

A shelf full of books!

Clara took down one book
and opened it.

There were so many letters.

There were so many words.

It made her dizzy.

32

"Well, well," said Mr. Holzer.

"So you want to borrow a book."

Clara looked up.

"How much does it cost?" she asked.

"It does not cost a cent.

It is a library book,"

said Mr. Holzer.

"My store is a book station."

"It does not cost anything

to borrow a book?"

Clara asked.

"That is right," said Mr. Holzer.

"The books are free of charge."

Clara ran to Papa.

"Papa, look!" she said.

"I can borrow a book free of charge.

I can learn to read."

Papa did not smile.

He put his arm around Clara.

"Books are for rich people,"
he said.
"Farm people like us
do not have time to read."
Papa put the book
back on the shelf.
Clara's eyes filled with tears.

Papa handed Clara

a peppermint stick.

"Here, Clara," he said.

"You almost forgot

your candy treat.

Come!

It is time to load the wagon.

It is time to start for home."

# 3   The Black Wagon

One summer day

Clara and Papa were weeding

the garden patch.

"Clara!" Mama called.

"I am going to make blueberry jam.

Would you like to pick the berries?"

"Oh, yes," said Clara.

She looked at Papa.

Papa smiled.

"You have been weeding

a long time," he said.

"I will finish this job."

Clara took the bucket

and ran

to the wild blueberry field.

She sang as she

picked the berries.

Suddenly she saw something

coming down the road.

It was a big, black wagon.

The wagon was pulled

by two horses.

A lady was driving it.

She waved and stopped.

Clara stared at the wagon.

It was filled with books.

"Hello," called the lady.

"I am Miss Mary, the librarian.

And who are you?"

Clara told Miss Mary her name.

"Did you ride all the way
from the city?" Clara asked.

"Indeed," said Miss Mary.

"Do you like our new
moving library?"

"Oh my, yes," said Clara.

"I never knew there were
so many books in the world."

Miss Mary said,

"We have books for the young.

We have books for the old.

And we have books
for people in between."

"Do you have any

for a girl like me?" Clara asked.

"Indeed," said Miss Mary.

"We have *Mother Goose* and

*Father Goose.*

We have *The Wizard of Oz*

and all the magic Oz tales.

We have *The Rabbit Witch*

and *Peter Pan* and

poems of every kind."

Clara could hardly say a word.

"Would you like to borrow a book?"
Miss Mary asked.
"You may keep it
until the next wagon trip."
"I wish I could," said Clara.
"But Papa says
books are a waste of time
for farm people."

"Nonsense," said Miss Mary.

"We will go and speak

to your Papa.

Climb up here."

Quickly Clara climbed up

onto the bookwagon.

# 4　Books for Clara

Giddyap! Giddyap!

Miss Mary got the horses moving.

Bump, bump, bump.

The wagon moved along

the dusty road.

How amazing! thought Clara.

I am riding on a bookwagon.

I am riding home on a bookwagon.

What will Papa think!

Bump, bump, bump.

They rode right up to

the garden patch.

Papa looked angry.

"You have made a mistake,"

he shouted.

"We have no dead here."

"This is not a hearse wagon

to pick up the dead," said Miss Mary.

"I am Mary Titcomb, the librarian.

And this is the first moving library."

Papa frowned.

"I bring books to people

who live in the country,"

said Miss Mary.

"Hummmph," said Papa.

"Our farm is not the right place

for a bookwagon."

"The wagon is for all farms,"

Miss Mary told Papa.

"Books are for everyone."

"We are too busy here," said Papa.

"Thank you and good day."

55

"Busy people must rest sometimes,"
Miss Mary said.

"Reading is good fun.
Reading can teach you new things
about your work, too."

Clara ran up to Papa.

"Please, Papa," she said.

Papa looked at Miss Mary.

"I know Clara wants a book,"
he said.

"But she does not know
*how* to read."

"If Clara wants to read,"

said Miss Mary,

"she will learn fast."

Papa lowered his head.

"Well, I...Mama and I...

we can only read a little," said Papa.

"I can teach Clara," Miss Mary said.

Clara tugged at Papa's sleeve.

"Please, Papa," she said.

"I will not read

until all my work is done."

Clara waited for Papa to answer.

At last Papa said,

"I know you are good

at keeping a promise."

"I am, I am," said Clara.

Papa sighed.

"All right, Clara.

You may borrow a book."

"Oh, thank you, Papa!"

cried Clara.

Clara ran to the wagon shelf.

"Miss Mary, will you

help me choose?" she asked.

"Indeed," Miss Mary said.

"Here is an alphabet book to start,

and a picture book of fairy tales.

I will show you

how to sound the letters."

Clara looked at the

alphabet book.

She looked at the

fairy tale book.

"Stories for me," she said.

"Stories for me to read!"

This story is based on the true account of the country's first traveling bookwagon. Soon after Mary Lemist Titcomb became head of the Hagerstown, Maryland, Public Library, she decided to make books available to the many people who lived far from the city. First she established small "book deposit stations" in general stores, churches, and homes throughout the sprawling county area. Then in 1905 she designed a horse-drawn wagon that could carry hundreds of volumes. The library janitor, Joshua Thomas, became the driver, who routinely covered 500 square miles of back-road territory.

The first "bookmobile" ran for five years, but was demolished when a train hit it at a railroad crossing. The driver and horses luckily were spared injury. By the time a new bookmobile was built in 1912, it no longer needed a horse to pull it. Maryland's second traveling library had a motor!

31901059270027